Amos's Sweater

BY
Janet Lunn

PICTURES BY
Kim LaFave

A Meadow Mouse Paperback

Groundwood/Douglas & McIntyre
Toronto/Vancouver/Buffalo

MOS was old and Amos was cold
and Amos was tired of giving away all his wool.

So one summer day when Aunt Hattie went out to the pasture with her big clipping shears, Amos balked.

"Baa," he cried. He butted Aunt Hattie. And ran away.

"Amos, stop!" shouted Aunt Hattie. "Stop, Amos!" But Amos did not stop.

Aunt Hattie ran after him. She chased him
around and around the meadow. She chased
him up and down the hillside and across the
brook. But Amos was too fast. Uncle Henry had
to help catch him and hold him down. Then
Aunt Hattie clipped his wool.

"There, now, Amos," she said. "That wasn't so bad, was it?"

"Baa," said Amos.

Aunt Hattie gave him an apple to make him feel better. But Amos did not feel better. He was old and he was cold and now he was angry.

Aunt Hattie washed the wool. She combed it and she spun it. Then she knitted it into a big, warm sweater for Uncle Henry.

"Isn't that fine, Amos?" She showed him the big, warm sweater.

"Baa." Amos snatched at the sweater with his teeth.

m Mc Allister

Every time Amos saw Uncle Henry wearing
his sweater he bit it. There were always Amos
holes in it that Aunt Hattie had to mend.

One hot day, when Uncle Henry left the sweater over the fence, Amos tried to pull it down. It stuck fast and he made such a huge hole in it Aunt Hattie came after him with a stick.

Aunt Hattie mended the huge hole. She
washed the sweater and hung it out to dry.
Amos waited for her to go back into the house.

Then he made a jump for it. But the line was
too high.

One night, Uncle Henry left the sweater
on the table in the back kitchen of the house.
The door was open. The moon was full. Amos
could see the sweater from his stall in the barn.

He butted the stall door. He shoved it. He
butted it, he shoved it. He butted and shoved
until the door flew open.

He dashed across the barnyard into the back kitchen. He yanked the sweater off the table. Furiously he pulled it this way and that. An end of yarn caught in his hoof.

He pulled and twisted to get it loose. He tugged. He twisted. He bit. He rolled around on the floor. The more he struggled the tighter the yarn wound around him. Soon he was so tangled you couldn't tell which was yarn, which was sweater, which was Amos.

"Baa," he cried, "Baa, baaaaa," in such rage
Aunt Hattie and Uncle Henry came running to
see what had happened.

"Oh, Amos. Now you've done it!" Aunt
Hattie sighed. Uncle Henry laughed. He began
to unwind the yarn. Amos glared at them with
his angry black eyes.

Free at last, he stood up. His two front legs were deep in the arms of Uncle Henry's sweater. His head poked through the top.

"You know, Hattie, Amos is old," said Uncle Henry.

"And maybe Amos is cold," said Aunt Hattie.

"And maybe," they said, both at the same time, "Amos is tired of giving away all his wool."

Now, if you go by the farm where Aunt Hattie and Uncle Henry live, you will see the sheep out in the pasture. There is one, standing a little apart. That is Amos.

He is old. But he is not cold because he is wearing his sweater.

For Peg, for Amos and for Ted,
with love

J. L.

For Carol and Jeffrey and baby

K. L.

A Meadow Mouse Paperback
Groundwood/Douglas & McIntyre
585 Bloor Street West, Toronto, Ontario M6G 1K5

Distributed in the U.S.A. by Publishers Group West
4065 Hollis Street, Emeryville, CA 94608

Canadian Cataloguing in Publication Data
Lunn, Janet, 1928-
Amos's sweater
ISBN 0-88899-208-4
I. LaFave, Kim. II. title.
PS8573.U55A8 1994   jC813'.54   C94-930510-3
PZ7.L85Am 1994

THE CANADA COUNCIL | LE CONSEIL DES ARTS
FOR THE ARTS | DU CANADA
SINCE 1957 | DEPUIS 1957

Groundwood Books gratefully acknowledges the assistance of the Canada Council and the Ontario Arts Council.
Printed and bound in China by Everbest Pritnting Co. Ltd.